Color Blind

To order additional copies, please contact us.
BookSurge, LLC
www.booksurge.com
1-866-308-6235
orders@booksurge.com

Color Blind

Phillip Woody

2006

Color Blind

Dedicated to my son, Cameron Scott Woody, whom I love dearly.
I could not have gone to the Creator and asked for a better friend. I am so very proud of you.

And to some great leaders which may or may not know how much they have touched my life:

Lieutenant General Robert Shea (USMC)
Lieutenant General Thomas Waskow (USAF)
Major General Ray Smith (USMC)
Brigadier General Ronald Coleman (USMC)
Brigadier Leif Hendrickson (USMC)
Colonel J. B. Beavers (USMC)
Colonel Walter Ford (USMC)
Colonel Christopher Iskra (USA))
Colonel Brian Manthe (USMC)
Captain "Woody" Woods (USN)
Mr. Marty Huisman GS-15
Lieutenant Colonel Gino Amoroso (USMC)
Lieutenant Colonel Michael Cordero (USMC)
Lieutenant Colonel Kevin "Buck" Rogers (USMC)
Lieutenant Colonel William G. Harris (USMC)
Sergeant Major Carlton Kent (USMC)

Sergeant Major Herve Saint Pierre (USMC)
Sergeant Major Eugene "Gene" Surface (USMC)
Master Gunnery Sergeant Anthony "Tony" Hicks (USMC)
Master Gunnery Sergeant James "Jim" Williams (USMC)
HM1 James "Jim" Beers (USN)

CHAPTER I

The Earliest of Life's Lessons

I remember it as if it were yesterday.

I couldn't have been more than six years of age. My family had been invited to my dad's boss's daughter's wedding. I needed hard-soled shoes. Being from the low country of South Carolina, shoes were not part of the daily ensemble, much-less hard-soled ones.

Momma and I caught a ride on the island ferry; walked to the bus stop; and took the bus into the city. Even though it was nine o'clock in the morning, it was hot. I mean blistering hot. Humidity was ninety percent, but it felt more like two hundred. Clothes would stick to you once you had been outside for less than two minutes. It was one of those days that if you took a shower in the morning and didn't hang up your towel, it would sour before nightfall.

We caught the bus at Hardee's Store, a small country store that had just about everything one could possible want. Momma and I sat on the front seat directly behind the bus driver. Because I had never been off the island, I am certain my eyes were as wide as could be with questions about everything being relayed and discussed as fast as my mouth could move. As we exited the bus, the bus driver asked my mom, "Does he ever not talk?"

The bus left us standing across the street in front of the Wade Hampton Hotel. The Wade Hampton was probably fifteen to twenty stories high; but to a little boy that had never seen a house bigger than "Old Man" Quattlebaum's, which was only three stories, it seemed like the biggest thing that had ever been created since the Tower of Babel.

Momma and I walked down Main Street to Tapp's Department Store. When we got inside I was amazed by all the stuff. The only store I had been in was Hardee's and I thought everybody in the world shopped at Hardee's. Imagine my surprise when I saw all newfangled hardware, clothes, and toys.

There was the prettiest woman I had ever seen standing in the window. She had on some of the fanciest and brightest clothes I could imagine. I was devastated when I found out she wasn't real. It took Momma twelve minutes to explain what a mannequin was. And when the sales-lady took off her arm to show me the lady wasn't real, I about wet my pants from fright.

I remember being intimidated by the new experience and all the commotion from the "ding-ding" of the intercom to the loud speaker calling for various people to come to different departments in the store. Momma stopped in several of the sections. She spent an inordinate amount of time in the fabric area. The lady behind the counter brought bolts and bolts of fabric out for Momma to see.

After we had been in the store for several minutes, I relaxed and became familiar with the coming and goings of the store. Some of the intimidation had worn off, and I felt comfortable enough to look around. While Momma was busy with the fabric lady, I wandered off to the backside of the fabric counter.

While on the other side of the fabric counter, I was amazed to see all the knick-knacks that were on display. I walked to the other side of the counter and found myself looking up and down a long aisle with white, shiny tile floors. Across the aisle was a small display of ladies' underwear. I had seen women's underwear before, but normally in the middle of the clotheslines' with two sheets strategically placed in order to cover the obvious from the neighbors' eyes.

Momma called out, "Phillip! Where are you?"

I replied, "Over here."

"Get back over here so I can keep my eye on you," she said. As I walked back over, she quickly finished her business and we moved on.

Momma had me by the hand, and we walked slowly since she would bounce back and forth from one side of the aisle to the other looking at the sales racks.

When we got to middle of the store, she made an abrupt turn and I came face to face with a hideous monster. It looked like a dragon with a metal tongue. Several people were already in the mouth of the dragon and were being swallowed. I screamed at the top of my lungs, "No, I don't want to go!"

She quickly snatched me up and away we went. While I was adamantly protesting, she reached up, popped my leg with her bare hand, and took care of that problem in short order.

At the bottom of the monster, we were delivered to a candy counter. A very young, pretty lady stood there handing out samples of candy. I can only imagine how I looked with my eyes swollen from crying, coupled with my gasping breath that came from being emotionally distraught, not to mention the solid handprint on my upper thigh. All these made the young lady reach out with a sympathetic gesture.

"Ma'am, can your son have a piece of fudge?" I didn't know what fudge was, but coming from someone so pretty it had to be good. I squirmed to get down and walked over to her to see what she had available.

Momma gave her half-hearted approval. As I got closer to the lady, she leaned over and said, "My name is Rachel. What's yours?" As I surveyed the numerous pieces of sweet concoctions on the doilied tray, I think I answered her. She asked, "Would you like one?"

Without hesitation I picked the biggest piece of fudge on the tray, shoved it into my mouth and said, as best as one could with a mouthful of fudge, "Thank-you!" At that moment, I immediately fell in love, not only with the heavenly treat in my mouth, but also with "Miss" Rachel. She smelled so good I can still remember it after all these years.

Momma held out her hand said, "Come on, let's go," and off we went again.

When we got to the bargain basement shoe department, an older gentleman who smelled funny walked up and introduced himself as Mr. O'Brien. He asked if he could be of any assistance. Momma stated that we were looking for boys' hard-soled shoes in black.

The man directed us to the back where there was a wall with a number of pairs of shoes in every size and color. He asked Momma if she knew what size I needed.

She indicated no, so he brought over a foot-measuring device, placed it on the floor in front of me, and asked me to stand. As he was measuring, Momma indicated she didn't care what the measurement was. She wanted something a couple of sizes bigger so I could get several months' wear out of them.

After taking the measurement, Mr. O'Brien excused himself by saying he would be right back with a couple of pairs for me to try on. I asked Momma, "Why does he smell so funny?"

She told me, "Be quiet and act like a young man."

After a short period of time, Mr. O'Brien returned with several boxes of shoes. I tried on the first pair and told Momma, "They are too loose and my foot slips around."

Momma reached into her purse, pulled out a piece of newspaper, wadded it up, and slid it into the toe of the shoe. She slid the shoe back on my foot and asked, "How does that feel?"

I told her, "Better, but it still moves up and down back here," pointing to my heel.

She told me to walk to the end of the row of chairs and back, and she asked Mr. O'Brien, "How much are those?" "Three dollars and ninety-nine cents without tax," he replied.

Momma and Mr. O'Brien went through every box of shoes, having me try on some and discarding the others. He went to the stockroom two more times looking for more shoes.

Finally, Momma decided on a pair of brown, laced shoes that were as hard as horseshoes and felt about as comfortable.

I remember the total was four dollars and eight cents, and Momma complained about us having to spend that kind of money. "We ought to tell them we can't go and leave it be," she said as she talked about the upcoming wedding. "We don't know them people anyway. He just wants to show the whole town how much money he has got. Sinful, just sinful," she continued.

It was very early in the afternoon and Momma asked if I was hungry. I had learned earlier in my life never to turn down food, because I never knew when or from where the next meal would be coming. On the same floor as the shoe department was a cafe. We walked up to the counter and took two seats. I had never sat in a chair so high and it also swiveled.

Ruby, the lady behind the counter, was a grandmotherly type who was trying to keep her good looks. However, she had already lost the battle; with big blue hair stacked on top of her head, gobs of make-up on, and the deterioration from years of having been a heavy smoker had obviously taken their toll.

Momma ordered a grilled cheese sandwich, a hamburger, a large order of fries and two glasses of water. I guessed the hamburger was for me since I didn't know what a grilled cheese sandwich was.

While Ruby was cooking our food, she and I had a nice

conversation about where we were from and my adventures in the city. When Ruby brought us our food, she asked Momma if it would be okay if she gave me a Pepsi on the house. Momma said, "I reckon so." As Ruby walked away I asked Momma, "What's on the house mean?" "Free," she responded.

Man, this was great! Pretty girls who smelled good handing out free candy and now a free Pepsi. I remember saying, "A boy could live here forever in total comfort."

After lunch, Momma looked at her watch and said, "It's time for us to leave. Our bus should be coming in a little bit. Are you ready to go?"

I was swiveling from side to side and didn't respond, hoping we could stay until supper. I guess Momma didn't want to go through the earlier fiasco of the escalator because while Momma was paying the bill, she asked Ruby for directions to the stairs. She directed us to the very back of the store. Again, Momma took my hand and off we went.

After we got to the top of the stairs, we headed straight for the exit. It was raining one of the summer afternoon showers so famous in the South. I could barely see the stores across the street as the rain poured down.

Momma looked at her watch and said, "It doesn't matter. We gotta go." With Momma still holding my hand, we walked out the door.

The rain was coming at us in a horizontal direction. It hurt as it slapped across my skin. The store awnings popped in the wind and I was scared. The streets were mostly deserted; and if we had not needed to get to the bus station, we would not have been out there ourselves. We waited under an awning until the traffic lights changed. Then we ran to the next street to the next store awning.

As we shook off the excess water, I saw a black man coming toward us in the opposite direction. Momma put me on the side farthest away from him and we continued to walk. When we got within ten yards of him, he stepped out from under the awning and stood in the street where the water was rushing to the drain. As we passed, I saw the strangest sight. He stepped off the sidewalk and into the storm drain. The water rushed over his feet. Once by him, I looked back and saw him step back onto the sidewalk, shake the excess water from his feet, and continue on his way.

I looked up at Momma and asked her if she saw that man get into the water. She said, "Yes!" I asked, "Why did he do that? That's kinda stupid, don't you think? " She stopped dead in her tracks, stooped down, looked me in the eye and said, "He's supposed to. He's a Negro!"

That was my first introduction to the lessons on southern bigotry.

CHAPTER 2

The Follow-On

I do not recall exactly when the concept of the racial divide was ingrained in my young and impressionable mind, but I remember several examples of racial hatred rearing its ugly head in my household.

As I got older and was able to venture out into the community and as my small town became more populated, I remember seeing the "Colored Only" signs at the stores and water fountains, and "them" having to sit in the balcony of the movie house. Black men and women well into their seventies called poor white folk in their thirties, "Sir" or "Ma'am." Education, status, and age had nothing to do with it. It was only the color of their skin that led to this obviously wrong and warped path of servitude.

Dr. Martin Luther King was scheduled to speak in Columbia, South Carolina. I was too young to understand the politics of the day and I was far from being educated or enlightened. I didn't understand what all the ruckus was about. Several of the leading citizens in the community warned about the "negroes" getting on their "high horse" and "raising Cain" because "he" was in town.

One morning, *The State Paper* had a picture of Dr. King speaking at another engagement in Atlanta with the caption of, "King to Speak at State Capital Tomorrow." The article indicated that Dr. King preaches, "Peace to his People and Non-

Violent Confrontation." This was to assist "them" in accomplishing the racial equality and social changes the "negroes" of the community sought.

My father was not a formally educated man, and he was afraid to speak publicly about any matters other than his job or his children. The politics of the day was one of those topics on which he always had an opinion; but he was not willing to discuss it with anyone. Because of his lack of education, he lacked the self-confidence to try for something more than being a mechanic at the brick mill. I guess having a family on the verge of poverty and being concerned about money for the next meal could have had something to do with him not taking more risks in life or more chances at bettering himself.

I asked him that evening why the people were so scared of Dr. King.

"It's not Dr. King," he replied. "It is the effects of Dr. King. You see, he comes into a city, tells the Negroes how bad they are being treated, and follows by telling them they should protest peacefully. Problem is, emotions get the best of both sides and all hell breaks loose shortly after he departs. White police get hurt; blacks get hurt or killed; and both sides get angry. Racial unrest, protest, and demonstration are left in his wake."

I want to believe deep down that my father agreed with the Civil Rights protests; but as an uneducated man in South Carolina, he was afraid to say so, especially when others were around. I say this because several weeks after Dr. King departed the area, one of the black men Daddy worked with was killed in a terrible accident.

I knew the man. He had been to the house several times to help Daddy. They called him "Boo." I didn't know his real name. When I asked, Daddy told me they called him "Boo" because he scared the hell out of everybody. I agreed. He was the biggest man I had ever seen and was very strong.

I remember him helping Daddy put shingles on a two-story house. Boo picked up four squares of shingles. I learned the term "square of shingles" from that week's work. Like a bale of hay or a bag of feed where everybody knows how much it weighs and what it is. A square of shingles weighed about 100 pounds.

He put two squares on each shoulder and then walked over to the ladder. Without holding on, he climbed to the roof of that two-story house and put those shingles down like they were feathers. I was very impressed, because I could not lift one square by myself.

The day before the accident, we had a terrible storm. Boo was helping cut down some trees that had fallen into a neighbor's yard as a result of the storm. Daddy said that Boo put on a safety harness and climbed a tree that appeared to be in a precarious position and which might fall on the house. He explained how the safety harness wrapped around the tree trunk and the person doing the cutting, allowing him to lean back for leverage with the chainsaw as he cut. We had heard that sometimes the tree would split in the middle causing the harness to pull the individual into the trunk, thereby crushing him.

As Boo started "topping" the tree, it split. Daddy said before Boo could release the safety harness and fall to the ground, it pulled him into the trunk of the tree and crushed him to death.

I could tell by the quiver and tone of Daddy's voice he was quite saddened by the tragic event. He had Momma go to the store and get a whole fryer chicken, cut it up, and fry for Boo's family. Fried chicken was normally reserved for Sunday dinners. If you got fried chicken and it wasn't Sunday, that meant something was horribly wrong. This was one of those times.

Daddy left with the chicken and came back later, visibly saddened by the tragedy. I could tell because his eyes were red and a little puffy. I had never seen my father cry until that day. I'm not certain as to the personal friendship he and Boo had, but I am certain they had a very close working relationship. Daddy sat in his chair, lit a cigarette, and said aloud, "That was a good Negro we lost today."

In today's political environment, we would cringe at such a statement; but in those days it was a great compliment. I asked Daddy if he was going to the funeral. He said he couldn't because he didn't want the people of the town to call him a "Nigger Lover."

My father is still alive today. When anyone brings up Boo's name, my father will perk up and tell a story about how he had done this or how he had done that; but he always finishes with, "Boy, I should have gone to his funeral to properly pay my respects to him and his dear family."

About the time I graduated from the fifth grade, segregation was outlawed and integration was being forced into the public schools. All the black students in the area went to one school. The whites went to two different schools: first through seventh grades in one and eighth through twelfth in another. The number of students had not increased. We had three different schools before and we still had three different schools; however, buses took some white students to the formerly all-black school, and took some blacks to the formerly all-white schools. The school system did its best to restructure in order to accommodate all the children. This meant the elementary school would become first through fifth grades; the black school would become a middle school educating all students in sixth through eighth grades; and the high school would house the ninth through twelfth grades.

On the night before I started the sixth grade, Daddy watched the local evening news intently. It was full of pictures of various protests going on at the local public schools across the South. Whites and blacks stood on both sides of the road shouting at one another over the racially charged issue. Several news commentators interviewed the people who were protesting. School integration appeared to be ineffective; it only fueled the fire of racial bigotry.

Daddy woke me up early the next morning. He told me to get dressed and come to the breakfast table. When I got there, he had made breakfast. He hadn't made breakfast since my little sister was born. I asked Daddy, "Did Momma have a baby?" He said, "No! Why?" "Cause you made breakfast. You never make breakfast." I could tell by his response that he was not amused. He said, "I just want to talk to you a few minutes before I go to work."

Daddy poured his coffee into a saucer as he always did so it could cool before he drank it. He tried to explain to me, the best his fourth grade education would allow, about the situation at school. He told me people would be there screaming and hollering. He told me not to pay attention to them; but to go into the school as fast as I could once I got off the bus. However, in case anybody looked like they wanted to hurt me, he gave me a pocketknife and showed me how to open it. He told me how to put my fingers on the blade and stab someone. "If you use this knife the way I'm showing you, you will not seriously hurt anybody, but it'll give you some time to get away and get help," he stated.

As all little boys do, I wanted my father to be proud of me. I wanted to show him how brave I was and assure him I wasn't scared. I am certain I answered in my toughest and deepest voice, claiming I would do something I couldn't possibly accomplish.

He was immediately angered and scolded me. "You'll do no

such thing. You get off the bus and you go into the school as fast as possible. Don't say anything to anybody and use this," he said pointing at the knife, "only if someone is on you or you're hurt. Do you understand me?"

A scared and respectful, "Yes, sir," followed.

Daddy continued getting ready for work, kissed me good-bye, and told me he would see me after work. When I got on the bus, the tension was already heavy. It was a forty-five minute ride to the school. This was another point of controversy. There were other schools located approximately fifteen minutes away, yet we rode the bus farther away to support racial equality.

Momma said, "Why we gotta bus these young'uns all the way up there? Why can't they go to that school up the road?"

As the bus got closer to the school, the children started singing, "Save your Dixie cups—the South's gonna rise again. Hey-hey-hey!!!" It was a catchy tune and easy to sing, but I am not certain how many of the children were singing out of protest and how many were singing because it was fun. By the time we pulled into the school driveway, every child was singing at the tops of their lungs. Looking back on that scene now, I see that the song was stupid and did nothing but add to the tension of the moment.

Hundreds of protesters, both black and white, were outside the school, and several police cars were stationed around the school. Once I got inside, there were no problems. However, the formerly blacks-only school was in deplorable condition. The wooden floors had holes so big a person could disappear into them; commodes were ripped out of the walls; sinks were missing; paint was peeling off the walls in long strips; desks were broken and piled in the back of the classrooms; blackboards were falling off the walls; and windows were broken or missing, with plywood covering some of the holes. It was frightening to see the condition of the school. If I didn't know better, I would have thought the building was abandoned. I thought, "This is unbelievable. No wonder blacks wanted equal rights if they had to be educated in a facility such as this."

CHAPTER 3

The Friend

Two years before I graduated from high school, I was dating a seventeen-year-old girl by the name of Helen who lived on an old, narrow, country road. The road ran under a very low bridge, no more than eleven feet high. I'm not sure exactly how high it was because there was no sign giving the clearance, no warning of any kind.

One day when I was at Helen's house, a fourteen-foot delivery truck made a wrong turn down Helen's road. The driver evidently was not familiar with the area and tried to drive the truck under the bridge; but it was too tall and became wedged under the bridge. The damage appeared minimal. The driver was a young-looking fellow with bushy, dirty blond hair and a thick mustache with some pink-tinted glasses. He was certainly emotional about being stuck and was in a quandary trying to figure out what to do.

Helen walked over to talk to the driver, who had already jumped on top of the truck to access the damage. She asked, "Are you the driver of this truck?" He belligerently replied, "No. I am the operator of this truck."

Helen didn't back down one inch. She was a wild child and certainly willing to take on "the establishment" against any cause. She was not very attractive, but was one of the smartest girls I had ever met. She said, "Well, what were you operating when this truck hit the bridge?"

He didn't even acknowledge her sarcastic comment. He was cussing and fussing about what his boss was going to do to him and how much it would cost for a wrecker. The driver jumped down, got into the cab, cranked up the truck, put it in gear, and tried to back the truck up. After grinding the gears and easing out on the clutch, he slowly gave it some gas. One could tell by the sights, sounds, and smells that the driver was getting more and more agitated by the situation. Faster and faster the engine roared, and faster and faster the tires spun; but his attempts to free the vehicle were fruitless.

With the air full of white smoke from the burning of the tires, and the smell from the transmission so pungent it would make a polecat run for cover, he got out of the cab of the truck just fuming. Helen hollered over at him, "How much room you reckon you'll need to get it unstuck?" He looked at her as if it were her fault and said, "Probably an inch." She looked him dead in the eyes and said, "Why don't you just let a little air out of the tires and lower the truck some?"

I thought that idea was on the verge of being near the certifiable genius scale. The operator got down onto the ground and let some air out of the front tires. Within five minutes the truck was low enough to be free of the bridge.

The driver didn't even show any gratitude. He just backed his truck up and went down the road. As he got onto the main drag and started off, Helen said, "I bet that operator will win a Nobel Prize for stupidity one day." I didn't even know what a Nobel Prize was, but I agreed with her.

Helen and I worked in the local outlet of a seafood restaurant chain, along with another guy a little older than we were. His name was Charles Valerie. Charles was the oldest of seven children and lived in Black Bottom. That was not the area's real name, but everybody called it that because everyone who lived there was black. Looking back at Charles, he was probably a little slow when it came to his intellect and this only added to the stereotypical thinking of the local community. His daddy was a long-haul truck driver and his momma stayed at home with the children.

One night I had to work a little later than Helen. She had gotten off work and was waiting for me in the car in the restaurant's parking lot. We were going go to the late movie together.

Charles walked out the side door of the restaurant near where Helen was sitting. He saw her in the car and he walked over and started talking to her. Just then, three farm-boy "red-necks" walked out of the pizza parlor next door and saw Charles talking to Helen. The tallest was a bearded man with long, stringy, reddish-colored hair. He walked over to her on the driver's side and asked her if she was okay. The other two men walked over to the passenger side of the car. Helen said she was fine, and explained that she was waiting for her boyfriend to get off work. With a scowl on his face, he pointed to Charles and asked Helen, "Is this 'boy' bothering you?"

Helen said, "No, he works here with me. We're just talking." He continued, "What would your Daddy think if he saw you out here with that 'boy'?" Helen, being her normal bold self, answered, "None of your damn business! Now get the hell outta here and leave us alone."

One of the other girls that worked with us saw the commotion and went inside to call the police. We were in a busy, upscale part of town and the police were quick to respond. Helen and the man were still arguing when the police pulled up. The police asked, "What's the problem here?"

Pointing at Charles, the bearded man explained that he thought that the black man was attacking the white girl. By that time, I had heard there was a problem in the parking lot with

Helen and Charles and stepped outside to see what was happening. Charles kept his eyes glued to the ground and didn't say a word. One could tell the police wanted to side with the bearded fellow, but the truth was Helen and Charles weren't breaking any laws.

The police told the farm boys to be on their way and took Charles over to the back of the police car. As the men drove away in their beaten up two-toned truck, one of the other men hollered out the passenger window, "I'm gonna find out where you live and teach you a lesson about white women, boy!"

The police told Charles, "Pay them no mind. Get yourself home where you belong, and don't be talking to any more white girls." Charles didn't say a word, just kept his head down and walked back into the restaurant.

Three days later Charles' Daddy called from Texas and told his wife he was not gonna be able to come home for the weekend and the closest he could get to the house was Charlotte, North Carolina. He wanted her to catch the bus and meet him there on Saturday. Charles asked to get off from work so he could watch the other children. He was always on time; never was disrespectful; and rarely asked for time off. Mr. Bailey, the manager of the restaurant, agreed to let Charles off on Saturday if he promised to come in early that Sunday to ensure all the clean-up close-out procedures had been accomplished Saturday evening. Charlie agreed.

On Saturday, Charles got his momma to the bus station and got all the children back home safely. That evening after supper, Charles heard his dogs barking; but didn't pay it much attention. He had put the children to bed and was getting ready for bed himself when a gunshot rang out. Charles bravely got all the children together in the baby's upstairs bedroom. Another shot rang out so Charles started down the stairs to see who it was and what they wanted. As he started to look out a window by the front door, he heard a window break in the upstairs hallway between him and the baby's bedroom where the children were. As he started back up the stairs, flames immediately engulfed that part of the upstairs. Charles grabbed a blanket off the living room sofa and tried to put the fire out, but it spread very rapidly. When he realized his attempts to extinguish the flames were in vain, he tried desperately to get back to the baby's bedroom to get the children out; but the heat was so intense he couldn't get through.

Charles hurried down the stairs, ran out the front door, and looked up toward the baby's bedroom window. He could see his younger brother trying to break the window. Charles ran to the shed to get the ladder, but by the time he got there, he heard his little brother screaming. As Charles rushed back to the house with the ladder, he heard all the children screaming, as they were being burned alive. Charles had hurried to get back with the ladder as quickly as he could, but by the time he returned, it was too late. The whole house was ablaze. The neighbors said they could hear the children screaming from a mile away.

Charles never recovered from this nightmare. He started drinking heavily and was fired from his job because of his inconsistent work pattern and erratic behavior. Before Helen and I graduated from high school, Charles was dead. He had hung himself from the rafters of the burned-out gutted house where his brothers and sister were burned alive. The police never discovered who started the fire.

Rest in peace, Charles, it wasn't your fault. You did the best you could.

CHAPTER 4

The Teacher

Being a Southerner by birth does not automatically make one a bigot. I never considered myself a racist or even disliked a person just because of their skin color until my freshman year at college.

I have never claimed to be a man of great intellect and my short stint at the university was my proving ground. There, at an institute of higher learning, I learned to think on a higher level and to look at everything from different perspectives.

Fridays were my short days. I had never actually reviewed the classes that were offered and the times the classes were available. I just turned in the courses I needed and the registrar provided me a schedule. By some miracle, I had a schedule that allowed me to leave at 10:30 a.m. on Friday and my next class wasn't until 9:45 a.m. the following Monday.

I had taken a class called "Religion Appreciation." It met on Wednesday evenings at 6:30 p.m. I didn't take this class because of my religious beliefs. I didn't even know what the course was about. I took this class because of Kathleen Marie Anderson.

Because she was a premature baby and very tiny at birth, Kathleen was nicknamed Tina. Tina was the most beautiful thing I had ever seen. She was a cheerleader in high school. Her looks and cute body automatically made people notice her. Men drooled and women who didn't know her hated her. She had a bouncy auburn coiffure, which lay, delicately around her narrow face, accentuating her high cheekbones. Her skin was so clear and fair that Walt Disney could have used her as a model for Snow White. Her eyes were as blue as the Caribbean Seas. She was not especially well endowed, but she knew how to wear clothes that made her look more developed than she was. She had a smile that was absolutely beautiful and she would blush when the wind blew. She was so cute when she blushed that guys would do their best to make her do so. And the coup de grace—the perfume. She wore a scent for which I would gladly pay a thousand dollars for quarter of an ounce today, if only I knew the name of it.

Tina and I had talked on occasion and I thought I might be able to get her to go out with me. I had taken the class in order to give her the opportunity to get to know me and to see if she might be interested in dating me.

The professor, Dr. Oscar Zeman, was as stiff as the starched collar on a man's shirt at the turn of the Twentieth Century. Everyone called him Dr. Oz. The first time I saw him, I noticed that he had an unusual gait. It was such an unusual walk, I am certain that as a child he must have been made fun of and bullied over that defect. Before he made it to his desk which was in the center of the lecture hall, I remember leaning over to Tina and saying, "This guy looks like he could bore a hole in a six by six in one class."

Tina snapped back, "Don't judge a book by its cover!" I thought that I might have ruined my chances in the first few minutes of the first class.

Through Dr. Zeman's lectures, I found out he was rejected by the military during the Korean War 4-F which meant for medical reasons. This was something he spoke about on two different occasions during the semester. One could tell he was disappointed in himself because he didn't have the opportunity to serve in the Armed Forces. Maybe because of that disappointment, he threw himself into his studies.

What a scholar he was! In my lifetime, I had never met anyone more enlightened and gifted than Dr. Oz. He asked questions which I thought God Almighty would have trouble answering. To listen and let him explain the intricacies of human beliefs, religious beginnings, and reasons behind physiological profiles of the human psyche, not only from that day's headlines, but any period in history, was an emotional experience. Whenever I left his classes, I was already looking forward to the next session. He truly had a talent that many professional educators wished they could emulate.

His classes were difficult, challenging, and mind-expanding. He made one think and work and reach outside oneself to find the answers to the questions he would ask. One of our assignments from Dr. Zeman was to separate into groups and visit at least three institutions of religious faith. The tasks were simple——visit a religious institution or organization during a normal service and witness the ceremonies, the liturgies, the sermons, and the rituals and report back our accounts of the sights and sounds. From these observations, we would discuss their meaning and origins.

One of the stipulations of this assignment was we had to get our list of institutions or organizations approved by Dr. Zeman before we could make any observations. At my insistence, Tina and I teamed up and decided to visit a Jewish Synagogue, a Greek Orthodox Service, and a Pentecostal Holiness Tent Revival meeting. When we took our list to Dr. Zeman for approval, he stated that no one had ever asked to go to a Pentecostal Holiness Church much less a Tent Revival Meeting. He surprised me when he asked if he could accompany us. I was more than honored to have him along.

The meeting was in a very rural part of the state, and it took us nearly two hours to get to the town where the revival meeting was to be held. We were not lost, but it took us longer to get to the meeting than we had originally planned.

When we got to the tent, it was full. An usher met us at the entrance, and escorted us to some folding chairs that were in the very front row. I had never been to a revival meeting and was looking forward to the experience.

Several events took place that were certainly beyond the scope of my comprehension. People were being anointed with oils; shouts of praise were being randomly bellowed out; people were holding up their hands to the heavens; some were speaking in tongues, and still others were translating this seemingly incoherent gibberish into something understandable. All the while it seemed to me to be semi-controlled chaos. Dr. Zeman appeared to be at ease with all the events.

Some of the older men lighted a fire and held their hands and faces so close that you could smell the singed hairs. One woman went into a convulsion fit and I thought she needed an ambulance; but I looked to Dr Zeman for some reaction and he was as stalwart as any man I had ever seen. The preacher shouted out verses from the Bible.

I'm not exactly certain what verse was quoted; but I remember vaguely him saying something to the effect, "Those who are witnessing and ministering the Word of God, who are bitten by an asp, who may be asking for salvation and reassurance and salvation and reassurance will be delivered. Thus saith the Lord!"

About that time some young boys brought in from the back of the tent three green boxes and placed them in front of the preacher. The preacher kicked off the lid of one of the boxes, reached down, and pulled out a handful of snakes. He walked down the center aisle of the big tent and repeated the Bible verse that he had just quoted. When he finished, "Thus saith the Lord", the preacher threw the snakes into the audience and went back for another handful.

This was an awkward moment. I am not afraid of snakes, but I can assure you I respect them a great deal. Tina, however, was so close to me that if she would have gotten any closer, she would have been wearing my clothes and I would have been naked.

Tina looked at me with tears in her eyes, scared half out of her wits, and asked me, "Where is the back door?" I told her, "I don't think they have one." With deep anguish in her voice she said, "Where do you think they would like one, because I am getting out of here!"

I looked at Dr. Zeman and told him I would meet him back at the car when the service was over. He patted me on the shoulder and said, "I will be there in just a few minutes."

He pointed me to the side aisle where we might be able to get to the back faster and safer. Anything was better than trying to go down the center aisle where we had entered, since it was filled with people and snakes.

When Tina and I got outside, she was absolutely beside herself. She was a nervous wreck and kept saying, "I never have seen such a sight. What did all that mean?"

She must have said it a hundred times. Dr. Zeman came out of the tent within a few minutes of us, and Tina was still asking the same questions. He said we would discuss it with the others when we got back to our class with the others next week.

However, the greatest lesson I was to learn from Dr. Zeman was yet to come.

CHAPTER 5

The First Lesson

Tina and I were still young and very impressionable. The tent revival events that had just unfolded before our eyes had taught us more than I could have ever learned in a month of solid studying at the Library of Congress.

Tina and I asked Dr. Zeman questions simultaneously. He was frugal with his responses and gave us very little insight as to the meaning of the rituals we had just witnessed. He kept repeating, "We can discuss it when we return to class."

As I drove down the desolate country road, I thought, "I certainly hope Tina doesn't think all southern people act that way. God, she would never date me if she thought I was anything like that!"

I looked in my rearview mirror at Tina who was sitting in the back. She had her hand covering her mouth and was staring out the window with tears in her eyes. I could tell she was still scared. I almost asked Dr. Zeman to drive so I could get back there with her and provide a little comfort.

I asked her, "Do you want something to drink?"

She immediately responded, "Please."

I passed a road sign which indicated the town of Gilbert was four miles ahead. Gilbert was so small it didn't even have a traffic signal. It did, however, have a convenience store.

I stopped and asked her what she wanted. She said, "Anything cold." "Dr. Zeman, how about you?" I asked. He reached into his pocket, pulled out a five-dollar bill, and said, "How about getting us each something cold to drink."

As I walked inside the store, I could hear someone arguing in the darkness and it sounded as if people were approaching the door. I went to the back of the store and got three Pepsis out of the refrigerator. As I opened the bottles, four young black men walked in and asked for some change for a one-dollar bill for the pay phone outside. I went up to the counter, paid for the drinks, and started for the car.

The four black men stood in front of my car. One of the men grabbed the pay phone, and I could hear the coins as they dropped into the slot. I didn't even acknowledge their presence, but I heard the man on the phone say, "Mom, there is something wrong with the car. It won't start."

I got into the car, handed Tina one of the drinks, and tried to nonchalantly lock the car doors, both hers and Dr. Zeman's. I handed Dr. Zeman his drink, and turned to put on my seatbelt, which I rarely if ever wore. I locked both doors on my side of the car. I slowly pulled out of the convenience store parking lot and headed for home.

I dropped Dr. Zeman off at the university and then took Tina home. Tina was still upset, and I thought it best not to try any smooth moves while she was in that state. I am not very wise, but I am a MOTO, which means for "Master of the Obvious".

When I got home I was so wound up I couldn't sleep. I was thinking about all the events of the evening and I sat down and tried to write out everything I remembered. I was looking forward to Dr. Zeman explaining everything in great detail not only to me, but also to all the others. I knew the next class would be a high-energy, learning experience.

The following Wednesday I arrived at the classroom a full

twenty minutes before class and reviewed my notes. Tina came in ten minutes before the class started. She and I started talking about our experience. As soon as the other students heard our conversation, they became equally enthralled by the evening's events. By the time Dr. Zeman arrived, Tina and I had already primed the others. We were all waiting to be inspired by the great, wonderful, all-knowing, and powerful OZ.

Everybody was seated and waiting for Dr. Zeman to explain the events and how they related to events in the Bible. He cleared his throat, looked at me and said, "Phillip, are you a bigot?"

What did that have to do with the tent revival? There were black people and white people at the event, I thought to myself. I looked at Tina with what I am sure was the most puzzled look I could muster, and said, "Sir?" as I looked back at him.

"Are you a bigot?" he repeated.

"No, sir, I don't think so," I replied.

"Then why did you lock your car doors the other night at the convenience store?" he asked, his voiced quivering with emotion. "If those young men had been white, would you have locked your doors?"

At that moment I had to ask myself the same question. *Am I a bigot?*

He continued, "How do you think those young men felt? If they would have been white, would you have offered to give them a jump or assist them with trying to get the car fixed?"

He looked at the rest of the class and provided them a full accounting of the evening's events at the convenience store. He rhetorically asked, "What would you have done? Why? And would you have done it differently if the young men were a different color?" The classroom which was one hundred percent white was deafeningly silent.

After that night I frequently asked myself, *"Am I a bigot?"*

I am certain Dr. Zeman provided an explanation to everything that took place in the tent revival, but for the life of me I cannot remember what he said about it. What I do did learn is colleges and universities are institutions of higher learning, and sometimes the most important lessons taught there are not in the books. On that night I had looked forward to hearing Dr. Zeman explain in layman's terms all of the sights and sounds that fundamentalist Christian group meeting. Instead, on that night I was provided one of the greatest lessons I have ever received.

I will always be very grateful to Dr. Zeman for making me take the time to notice and pay attention to the little things I do that affect those around me. He made me look deeply into myself to see the true me in a light I'd never before seen.

Aristotle wrote many years ago, "The only way for a mortal man to become immortal is to teach, for those that are taught will pass on the teacher's name and the lessons that were provided and the teacher will remembered forever."

Dr. Zeman will always be a part of my life. He passed away in 1984 and, in my opinion, the world is not the same without him. It is hard to believe that a man from humble beginnings who worked so hard to overcome a physical disability could teach so much to one who had an open mind.

Did I tell you Dr. Oscar Zeman was black?

CHAPTER 6

The Vagrant

The next year, Tina did not come back to school. I don't know why. I had heard that her mother was ill and she decided to stay home to rear her siblings. I tried to call her on several occasions. I would leave my number with a message, but she never returned my calls. I can only assume her feelings for me were not as strong as my feelings for her.

School was going well and I had found a job at the shopping mall in a well—known shoe store. It was an easy job. The store had very little traffic except on Saturdays, and the manager let me set my own hours as long as I worked Saturdays. He was a graduate student and understood the struggling student profile.

The best part of the job was the people that worked in the mall. Everybody knew everybody else, and we all had a symbiotic relationship. If I was hungry, I could call over to Taco Bell and talk to Kathy or Kevin and one of them would bring me something to eat. If I needed some clothes, I would go to the Levi Strauss Store and talk to Lisa, the manager, and she would go to the rack, get something that fit me, say that the garment was damaged, give me a huge discount, and then sell it to me with the employees' twenty percent discount. I could walk out of the store with a pretty fancy set of duds for less the twenty dollars. If I had a date, but little to no money in my pocket, which was often, (the no-money part, not the date part), I could always count on Darrel at Cromer's Peanuts to provide a snow cone, a bag of popcorn, or boiled peanuts to assist with the evenings. The best part was that right outside Cromer's, there was a small fountain with colored lights and a bench where people could sit. It was an inexpensive date and one would be surprised how loving and sensitive a man and woman can get over a bag of boiled peanuts.

Jackie worked as the bar manager at The Silhouette. She was only twenty-three years old, but because of her heavy life style, she looked and acted much older. The Silhouette was a typical hole-in-the-wall, college town, combo restaurant-bar-game room-hangout for most of us who worked in the mall. We always got happy hour prices no matter the time of day. We had our own special place to sit, and the girls who worked there knew what the prices were and how to work the register to get us discounts on food and drinks. I remember one night at two o'clock in the morning, seven of us walked out of the bar after six straight hours of merriment and the whole bill was $16.95. Jackie would provide coins out of the register that had been painted with fingernail polish so the game vendor would return them without taking it out of the fifty/fifty split on the business deal.

Most weeknights the bar had something special going on. Mondays and Tuesdays were amateur nights at the microphone so most people sang or played an instrument on those nights. Wednesdays were "unusual talent" nights. The most unusual talent I ever saw was a woman who could write Greek and Latin simultaneously. She would write Latin with her left hand while writing Greek with her right and she could change back and forth on command. I was very impressed. Thursdays were comedy nights. There was always a cash prize for the evening's best talent no matter which night or what was scheduled. On Fridays and Saturdays, a live band played on the small stage in the back of the bar. Normally the bands were not very good, but it was a place for them to practice and make a couple of bucks. And, live bands always seemed to bring in the girls.

The bar was always crowded no matter when you went. The food was greasy but very tasty and, most importantly, it was cheap and/or free if you worked in the mall. Most of the time the prize for the best talent was fifty dollars; but on occasion, depending on the quality of talent and the size of the crowd, it would be one hundred dollars. I never really thought of myself as a comedian, but my friends thought I was funny and always encouraged me to get up and tell a few jokes. For the longest time, I refused because I didn't want to purposely embarrass myself in public. I normally did a fine job of doing that without any advance planning. However, one night the crowd was going strong and the contestant I followed had not been very good so I thought I had a good chance of winning.

When I got on stage, everything clicked. I was so funny I was laughing at my own jokes. The best jokes were those that were short or considered one-liners. The more jokes you could put together in one minute, the more reaction you got. Once you got the crowd rolling, if you could keep the momentum, it was easy to keep them laughing; but the hard part was getting the momentum. I had been going to the club for the better part of a year and I knew the typical crowd liked jokes with racial overtones. I told a few of those jokes to get the ball rolling and then went into some of my own material or repeated some of the funnier jokes I had heard over the course of my tenure at the club. I did pretty well and won the one hundred dollar prize.

From that night on, I went to the club every Thursday and nine times out of ten I won the prize. This ritual continued until November. That was the month when my whole world was shattered.

The place I lived in could be, and had been described as, a shack from a third-world suburb. It was supposed to be a three-bedroom house, but every room was a bedroom. We had no less than six different sleeping rooms in the house. I am not certain how many different people lived there, but the numbers were high and the rotations frequent. It was not unusual to go to bed by yourself and wake up with a bunkmate. Normally, it was someone you had met before at a previous engagement or a friend of somebody you already knew.

I knew the house was infested with rodents. I got Jackie from the bar to let me have some of the rat poison she used there. She claimed the stuff was strong but it was as strong as a magnet for them, not as a repellent. I saw more rats after I had put it out than I had before. Several of the other residents complained also, stating they were seeing more evidence of rats, their destructive behavior, and their droppings.

The beginning of the end came about four in the morning on November 1st. We had held a Halloween Party at the house so several of the invited and uninvited guests slept over. Suddenly one of the girls let out a blood-curdling scream. Everybody was immediately on their feet, hangovers and all.

"What's going on in here?" Mike, the senior resident, asked.

Donna, the girl that screamed, pointed to her toe which was bleeding and hollered, "A rat just bit me!"

All the guys looked at one other as all the girls left. This called for immediate and decisive action. A whisper went up from those remaining in the house, "How much will it cost to get a professional exterminator to take care of this?"

Mike started calling exterminators bright and early the next day. Unfortunately, they all seemed to want money up front or else were booked up for most of the month. The earliest he could book anyone was November 12 at 10 a.m.

On Friday, November 12, we were all waiting by the door at ten o'clock for the exterminator. He got there at exactly 10:04 and 14 seconds. Mike explained the situation and showed the exterminator around the house. The exterminator's name was Joseph, according to the sewed-on nametag on his blue-and-white-striped shirt.

Joseph first examined the attic and didn't look concerned. He said he saw some evidence of a small infestation but he wanted to see the crawl space under the house before he provided an estimate.

We took Joseph out back to the crawl space door. He went back to his truck, put on some overalls, and came back within a few minutes. He opened the door, knocked down the cobwebs and crawled head first inside.

He couldn't have been gone for more than a minute before he came scurrying out screaming like a wild banshee. He went to his truck in such a hurry that we didn't get a cohesive sound out of him. When he got to the truck, he called on a radio back to the office. We asked Joseph what the problem was. He said we had one of the worst infestations of rats he had ever seen in seven years of exterminating.

We all asked, "Can it be eradicated?"

He said, "I don't know."

Within thirty minutes, two other exterminator trucks from the same company were at the house. Two men got out of each truck and the eldest man put on some overalls and went under the house. After five minutes he came out and asked if he could use the phone. He called the Department of Health and asked them to send an inspector.

An hour later, Mr. Don Davis from the Health Department arrived at the house. He asked some general questions about who owned the house, the age of the house, the number of occupants in the house, and how long the house had been constantly occupied.

Mr. Davis suited up in a white cloth over-suit with a paper mask. He looked like something off the evening news, reporting chemical spills at the neighborhood nuclear factory. He crawled under the house and was gone about ten minutes. When he crawled out, he was a little green around the gills and said, "This house is condemned effective immediately."

The infestation was enormous. He estimated 5000 to 7000 rats were residing under the crawl space of the house and the house possibly had to be completely destroyed in order to eradicate them.

It took a while for the ramifications to sink in. I was on the street, homeless and a vagrant. Worse than that, trying to find affordable accommodations that late in the school year would be impossible. I cleared my belongings out of the house that afternoon and put them in my vehicle. I drove around most of the afternoon trying to formulate a plan. I got on the phone and called several people who I thought were good friends, but I couldn't get one soul to let me sleep in their house. They were either gone, had someone already staying with them, or had a roommate that said, "No!"

I couldn't even get one person to let me spend one night. One would have thought I brought the rats into the condemned house myself.

That was a predicament I never planned on. I drove my car to the parking lot of the athletic practice field. I knew the place would be open so I could take a shower and possibly catch a nap on one of the sofas in the practice room.

After showering and cleaning myself up, I looked in the

paper for another apartment. Every place I called had already been taken or was way out of my price range.

Boone, a black custodian, saw the lights on so came in asking me why I was there and what I was doing. I explained the situation, but he did not have a sympathetic bone in his body. He told me to get out and never come back, and if I did he would call the campus police and have me arrested. I left, but not without throwing a few choice words his way first.

For the next few nights I stayed in my car. Trying to stay warm on winter nights in South Carolina is a very difficult job; however, I tried to make the best of a terrible situation. I was trying to keep up with my studies; but that meant keeping the car's dome light on for hours and a car battery would only last so long. I planned and executed some covert operations which involved some selective interchange of car batteries with vehicles located in the same vicinity as mine over the next few days. November 16th was without a doubt the coldest day since weather records had been kept. I literally nearly froze to death that night. I could not have endured another night like that in such severe weather.

It was then that Dr. Zeman once again had an effect on my life. As I considered my options, I started thinking about Dr. Oz and how he'd been rejected by the armed forces. Then the light bulb went on———join the armed forces. Absolutely, I decided, I'll go in the morning and see if I get turned down like Dr. Oz.

CHAPTER 7

Not In Charge

Morning couldn't come fast enough. The second coldest night since records were kept in South Carolina was the night before I went to the recruiting station. I was at the door, shivering from the cold when the first recruiter walked in just before 8 o'clock.

Sergeant Benny Fort was in civilian clothes. He could tell I was cold and asked, "Do you want to come in while I change into my uniform?" He was gone only a few minutes. As I stood there still shivering from the cold, I started looking at the propaganda on the walls. There was a poster of a Drill Instructor yelling into a recruit's ear with the caption, "We never promised you a rose garden." I thought it was funny and started to laugh to myself. Behind the recruiters desk was a picture of a Marine in his dress blue uniform with some small writing underneath the picture. I moved over behind the desk so I could read the information. The pictured Marine was a Congressional Medal of Honor recipient and the writing told the story of his actions in Vietnam which led to the presentation of his award to his family. When he came out, he said, "I keep it there for motivation. That man saved my father's life. Now, how can I be of assistance?" I told my whole story and said I wanted to enlist in the Marine Corps.

"Whoa! Just a minute," he said. It was funny to watch his expression. From his reaction, I am certain that I was a rarity.

For someone to walk in off the street and want to enlist in the Marine Corps must have been a real surprise.

He told me I had to take a battery of tests to see if I could academically make it in the Corps. He gave me the test and told me I had 45 minutes to complete it. He spoke slowly like I had some sort of a learning disability: "Pleeeeease reeeeead aaaallll instruuuuuuctions befoooooore begiiiiiinning the teeeeeeest. Iiiiiiii'll be oooooooout frooooooont iiiif and wheeeeen you are dooooone. Dooooon't wooooorry if you doooooooon't fiiiiiin-ish."

He still had that look of disbelief on his face after I handed him the paperwork twenty minutes later. He removed an answer key to the test from a file cabinet and checked my test against it. I had missed only one question.

Still with a look of hesitation on his face, he asked, "Do you have any physical problems that will prevent you from passing a medical exam?"

I answered, "No."

With the same look he asked, "Would you be able to pass a mental competence test, let's say, if one were to be administrated to you later today?"

"Yes," I replied.

"How about, let's say, in the next few days?"

I told him, "Look, Sergeant Fort, I know this is strange; but I really want to join the Corps. I know you don't have people walking in every day asking to join; but I am physically, mentally, and emotionally stable and I want to enlist in the Marine Corps."

He looked at me and said in a very stern voice, which he raised just a little, "When is the last time you had a drink?"

"I'm not drunk," I said.

He took a breath and looked a bit more relaxed. "When would you like to go to boot camp?" he asked.

"As soon as possible would be the best for me," I said. I thought I was going to have to pick him up off the floor.

He reached under his desk, grabbed some forms, and started typing. He was very happy. I could tell because every few minutes he would say, "The guys aren't going to believe this when I tell them a Class I just walked in off the street." As he continued to type, he would have to stop to find some information or ask me a question. Every time he stopped he would repeat, "The guys aren't going to believe this when I tell them. A Class I just walked in off the street."

The earliest I could get a seat was going to be ten days later. Even though I told him I wanted to leave immediately, that delay would actually give me time to get some personal things done before I completely altered my life.

The next ten days flew by as I sold my car, said good-bye to several friends—mostly girl friends, and gave away many things that I thought I would never need again. My tennis racket, my old sneakers, some old books, some clothes, and probably one of the most important things in my life—my "Pabst Blue Ribbon" neon sign which I had stolen from the college bar——all these were given away. Once that neon sign was gone, there would be no turning back!

Anyone who entered the military understood that boot camp was supposed to present life-altering experiences, but you can't imagine just how life-altering until you have actually been there and done it.

I went to boot camp at Parris Island. In the Marine Corps, this is a big deal. There are only two places for one to obtain the knowledge required to become a Marine: Parris Island, South Carolina and San Diego, California. Of course, in Marine discussions about which is the better, it's always the one you attended.

Parris Island is located on the coast of South Carolina. The natives refer to it as the low country of South Carolina. I was born and reared in South Carolina so I was quite accustomed to the heat and the humidity of the summer and the cold nights of the winter.

I am not certain if the 0200 arrival to Parris Island was by design or just the way it worked out for me. I think they do that purposely so the recruits do not know the way off the island. The bus that took us to Parris Island from Charleston, South Carolina, arrived in the wee hours of the morning.

A Marine sergeant got on the bus and, with great passion and emotion, explained what we were going to do, how we were going to do it, and at what speed we would be accomplishing this task. Later that day, we got our uniforms, got our heads shaved, got something to eat, went to sleep, and received what they called bucket issue.

Now, let me explain "Bucket Issue." We received our toiletries, towels, shower shoes, war gear (including, but not limited to two canteens, one first aid kit, magazine pouches, war belt, field jacket, field pack, and helmets) as well as other items required for the upcoming training.

After all of the initial administrative requirements were accomplished, we met our drill instructors. The Marines we had been working with thus far were receiving personnel. Other than an occasional outburst of emotions when someone messed up, they had been pretty tame; but then we got to meet the *real* drill instructors.

During the march to the new and permanent barracks, the Receiving Sergeant started with the mind games. "Oh, you recruits are in trouble! Y'all got Staff Sergeant Boyd as a drill instructor." This remark increased the already considerable tension among the new recruits by several times over. The Receiving Sergeant marched us down to the barracks where we would be billeted. As we arrived at the 3rd Battalion "H" Company, he continued his taunting, "Staff Sergeant Boyd. Oh my God! I'd hate to be you!" As we arrived at the barracks, an ambulance pulled up with sirens blaring and lights flashing. It stopped directly in front of the platoon. The back door flew open and out came Staff Sergeant Henry Lucas Boyd. He was a very large black man with a square jaw and one of the biggest heads I'd ever seen. He stood approximately 6 ft. 3 inches tall. He had no hair; I guessed that he shaved his head. His bicep was as big as my thigh, at least 22 inches around. He was wearing a loosely fitted straitjacket, screaming like a wild man in an insane asylum, and flailing around like a chicken with its head cut off. Recruits were running trying to stay out of his way as he wiggled out of the jacket. He appeared to be frothing at the mouth like he had rabies. I was way in the back and had a great vantage point from which to observe the show and was thanking my lucky stars my last name started with "W" which allowed me to be placed in the rear of the formation. I didn't want to be really close.

Recruits were moving around like ducks on a pond running from a fox. It was quite a spectacle, but then again I was way in the back so I was far removed from the action. After just a few minutes, he pulled the straitjacket over his head, threw it to the ground, and kicked it in the direction of the ambulance. He was still foaming at the mouth; but he calmly walked over to the ambulance, picked up his hat which was fondly called a "Smokey" cover because it looks like the hat worn by Smokey the Bear, and placed it gently on his head. When he turned around, he was still foaming at the mouth. He kept his eyes focused on us, but turned his head to spit.

In a clear, deep, loud voice he introduced himself as Staff Sergeant Boyd. He continued by saying, "For the next thirteen and one half weeks I will be your drill instructor. That means I will be your momma, daddy, sister, brother, aunt, uncle, Dear Abby, and your nemesis!"

I didn't know what a nemesis was, but I knew it couldn't be good.

He continued, "Every time I talk, you will listen. If when I speak it requires some audible grunts from you, the first word I will hear from your pie hole will be, 'Sir'. Once you grunt an appropriate response, the last thing I will hear from your pie hole is, 'Sir'. Do I make myself clear?"

A scared and low-keyed, "Sir, yes, sir," came as a response.

And just like on TV, he bellowed, "I can't hear you!"

Everyone responded in a loud scream, "Sir, yes, sir!"

It was obvious Staff Sergeant Boyd had been well trained and took to heart the mission of turning "slimy, unworthy, undisciplined, pig-foddered civilians" into "lean, mean, fighting Marines." Immediately, he took a bunch of out-of-control teenagers and started to mold us into a cohesive unit. I could tell he didn't like me. I don't know how or why I felt this way, I just did. I tried to do everything he asked to the very best of my ability, but I couldn't help but think he had a deep dislike for me.

Once while my platoon was on mess duty, I was working in the salad room making salads for the Officer's Mess. This was really a great job until I made a fatal error in judgment—I ate a crouton.

Now, let me explain my stupidity. Mess Duty was in the middle of the 13-week training cycle. The drill instructors had been with us every minute of every day for the previous six weeks. The mess and maintenance week was supposed to be a break for the Drill Instructors and a break for the recruits from the Drill Instructors. We rarely saw them, because the Marines, all of them cooks who ran the Chow Hall, were supervising us.

I don't know if it was because of the easy job, the lack of constant supervision, or just plain ignorance; but I ate a crouton. We were setting up for the noon meal. I was putting the vegetables in the refrigerated salad bar. I needed to get a serving utensil from the salad "prep" room which was in the back of the Chow Hall. As I walked by the huge bowl of croutons sitting at the end of the salad bar, I grabbed six or seven of the tiny little morsels of stale bread which had been toasted to a golden brown. I couldn't just pop them in my mouth and go about my job. Oh, no! I had to throw them in the air and catch them in my mouth like popcorn at the theater before the movie starts.

And then the worst thing that could have happened, happened! Staff Sergeant Boyd appeared out of nowhere. It was as if he was hiding just waiting for me to make a mistake, and bam, there he was. I had a crouton in mid-air, my mouth agape. Because my entire attention was focused on catching it, I ran smack into Staff Sergeant Boyd—my face to his chest.

He took me to the receiving dock in the very back of the Chow Hall and worked me with incentive physical training like there wasn't going to be a tomorrow. It was so cold I could see my breath as I started the intensive physical training. "Side-Straddle Hop! Push-ups! Mountain Climbers! Leg Lifts! Bends and Thrust!"

Over and over, faster and faster. I don't know how long I was out there, but when I stopped there was a huge pool of sweat under me and I was soaked. Some famous dead Marine whose name escapes me, once said, "The more you sweat in training, the less you bleed in war." Judging from that pool of sweat on the ground, I doubted I could ever be wounded in combat.

Staff Sergeant Boyd walked over close to me, leaned over

to my ear, and whispered, "Your character can only be judged by the things you do when others aren't looking." I understood exactly what he meant and went back to my duties; very proud of the lesson I had just learned. I watched Staff Sergeant Boyd a lot closer after that lesson. He was not only a professional Marine; but he had character, integrity, honor, and a commitment to duty. He was always the first Drill Instructor to come into the barracks, always the last to leave at night, and frequently, as we prepared to hit the rack, he would inspire us with stories of past warriors and feats that had been accomplished under the most hostile of environments. As training continued, I came to honor, respect, and even love this warrior. I thought he was the best Drill Instructor God had ever created.

CHAPTER 7 1/2

The Rest of the 13 Weeks

We were in our tenth week of training when a number of the recruits starting receiving "Dear John" letters. Staff Sergeant Boyd tried to keep the spirits up of all the recruits who had received such letters. It was obvious some took the news better than others. One of the recruits who took the news especially hard was a private by the name of Serifan. No one had a first name in boot camp.

I speculated that Private Serifan took the news so hard because he was as ugly as homemade sin. Not only was he ugly; but also he was skinny, spoon-chested, and weak with a high voice. He was not very athletic and certainly not one of the sharpest tools in the shed, but he really tried hard to accomplish each and every task. He had been recycled to my platoon. This meant he failed an earlier part of the training and had to go back to make it up

There was nothing in the world worse than being recycled, because it meant you had to stay on Parris Island longer than thirteen weeks. The Drill Instructors knew that. Anytime you screwed up—or even thought about screwing up—they would threaten recycling.

I was assigned the fire watch three days after Serifan received his "Dear John" letter. For two hours, I had to walk inside the barracks and ensure no fires started. It was actually to ensure no one went up to smoke; but under the guise of military training, it served its purpose.

It was just a few minutes past 0300. Staff Sergeant Boyd had the duty drill instructor watch. This meant he had to stay all night in case of an emergency. I knew the exact time, because every hour on the hour when Staff Sergeant Boyd had duty we had to bang on the "Drill Instructor's hut hatch"—his door—and yell out the time. I had just banged on the hatch and yelled out, "Sir, the time on deck is 0300, Sir!"

As I was returning to the squad bay where all the recruits were sleeping, Private Serifan walked past me going to the head. I continue to walk up and down the squad bay. I had one more hour to go and then I could get another hour of sleep myself. As I walked back down toward the head, I heard a crying noise. I walked into the head and Serifan had cut his wrist open and blood was gushing from his arm. Somehow I got to Staff Sergeant Boyd's hatch, knocked and hollered, "Sir, Private Serifan is in the head trying to commit suicide!"

Staff Sergeant Boyd immediately stepped out of the Drill Instructor hut as if he had been already standing by the door. He was fully dressed and awake. In a stalwart calm voice, he asked, "Where is he?"

I pointed toward the head.

"Show me," he continued. Staff Sergeant Boyd was calm and cool. If he was emotional, it did not show it. He was steady and reassuring in his approach.

He asked Serifan, "Son, are you all right?"

Serifan responded through the tears, "I don't want to live like this anymore. I just can't live like this."

Staff Sergeant Boyd took off Serifan's t-shirt and applied direct pressure to the gash. The blood had stopped gushing but was still coming out at a fevered pitch.

I asked, "Does this private need to call someone?" We were not allowed to use pronouns to describe ourselves and always had to talk in the third person.

Without emotion in his voice he replied, "No, I have already pushed the distress button." I didn't even know there was such a thing, but I was glad they had one.

Staff Sergeant Boyd was talking to Private Serifan as if he were his own son. "Russell, you have so much to live for," the sergeant was saying. "You are young, bright, and have so much to offer the world. It would be a shame for you to be so selfish to take what you have to offer away from the rest of us. I know you have a great deal going on in your life at the moment, but you must understand these problems are only temporary. You have chosen a permanent solution for this temporary situation. I believe together we can come up with an alternate solution. Are you willing to work with me on this?"

Private Russell Serifan sat on the toilet very calm as Staff Sergeant Boyd was reassuring him and continuing to hold direct pressure on the wrist. Serifan started to explain all of the troubles he had in his life. Before he could open his mouth, Staff Sergeant Boyd started speaking. "You have a car note which is due and no money to pay the note. Your girlfriend left you for somebody named 'Harold'," he raised his voice like a little girl as he pronounced the name "Harold." That brought a smile to Serifan's face. "You are scared of the next phase of training. And most of all, you want to get home so you can see Deena, your girlfriend."

Listening to Staff Sergeant Boyd talk to Private Serifan, it seemed he could read his mind. The man cared so much and had so much passion, not only with his chosen profession, but with everything he did. I remember after everything had calmed down and Private Serifan had been taken to the hospital, I was lying in my bunk and I thought, "I hope I can be as good at being a Marine as Staff Sergeant Boyd."

CHAPTER 8

The First Encounter

Graduating from boot camp was a wonderful feeling. I actually felt as if I had accomplished the impossible. The first time I was called "Marine" gave me a sense of euphoria. I was an invincible nineteen—year-old, ready to conquer the world.

Marines who graduate from boot camp get ten days' leave before they are required to report to their "Military Occupational Skills" school. During those ten days of leave, I went home to visit family and friends. I could tell my father was proud of my accomplishment.

My father and I were not very close as I was growing up. He was always at work trying to keep food on the table, and when you are working for a few cents above minimum wage with four children, it is difficult to keep meat and potatoes on the table.

We spent a number of hours together during the next ten days talking about my experiences in boot camp and comparing them to his time in the Army when he was drafted during the Korean Conflict. When I was smaller, he never discussed his Army career. As a matter of fact, even though I knew he had served, I didn't know when or with whom. It was great to finally be acknowledged by him as a man.

I left home and headed for Montford Point, near Marine Corps Base, Camp LeJuene along the coast of North Carolina, where the Marine Corps Service Support Schools were located. Montford Point used to be the boot camp for blacks when we had a segregated service. The place was old and dilapidated and certainly not what anyone would consider Marine Corps standards. However, they had turned the facility into a school. Several different service support schools had their initial training located at Montford Point. Motor Transport School, Administration School, Financial Accounting School, and Public Affairs all used Montford Point as their home base.

In boot camp, I was assigned the military occupation of supply clerk. Some of the Marines with whom I had gone to boot camp were now with me for the coming seven weeks of intensive training. Many excellent instructors would teach us the intricate supply systems and accounting procedures. Every day when we entered the classroom we had to recite the poem, "A Horseshoe Nail", written by Benjamin Franklin.

For the want of a horseshoe nail, the horse was lost.
For the want of a horse, the rider was lost.
For the want of a rider, the battle was lost.
For the want of a battle, the kingdom was lost.
All for the want of a horseshoe nail.

The poem provided the perspective that what we were doing was important. In boot camp, recruits had no time to themselves and certainly not for something called "liberty". In supply clerk school, we were treated as Marines and were expected and directed to act as Marines. Those of us assigned to the supply school had our first weekend of liberty since joining the service. We got out of school on Friday at 1630, 4:30 in the afternoon, and were not required to return until 0600 Monday morning.

Everyone had a meal card entitling him or her to eat at the chow hall for free, but that Friday we decided to go into town for dinner. No one had a car and there were too many to pile into a taxi so we walked to Sonic Burger.

Everyone ordered, got their food, and went to a booth over by the window to eat. I was sitting on the inside of a booth closest to the window. As I was eating, laughing, and joking with the others, I saw him out of the corner of my eye. He got out of a taxi with two other black Marines. I could tell they were Marines. Everyone everywhere was a Marine.

He stood about 6 feet tall. He looked as if he had just gotten a haircut. He wore a turtleneck sweater and a black leather jacket. He had a shadow over his lip, as though he was trying to grow a mustache.

His size allowed him to command attention, but what struck fear in the hearts of men was his look. He had a large scar over his right cheek that went up to his forehead right over the middle of his eye. I had no idea how he got the scar, but I am certain he was lucky to still be seeing out of that eye. The scar must have been there for some time since he walked with great confidence and without a bit of reservation. Apparently, he had grown accustomed to his obvious facial disfigurement.

His hands were big and just by looking at them; one knew that he was a motor transport mechanic. His knuckles were scraped from his work and his fingernails had grease under them. One could tell he had tried to remove the grease from them, but his efforts had been in vain.

We had all been told by our mommas not to judge a book by its cover, but it was difficult to look at him and not pass immediate judgment him. He was a big brute who used his muscle and brawn to leverage his wants and needs out of others and probably didn't have enough brains in his head to conjugate a verb.

I didn't know him, but I could tell I didn't like him and

that he was trouble. His look, his walk, his dress, and his mannerisms, everything about him in my opinion was distasteful, and he did nothing to change my mind or those in his sight. It is hard to admit now; but as I reflect on that moment, I probably was a bigot then. I had judged him without asking one question and came to a conclusion without understanding.

I wanted to get a better look at him; but much to my disappointment, neither he nor his friends entered the Sonic Burger Restaurant. As they walked past our window, our eyes met. Not wanting him to think I could be easily intimidated, once our eyes locked neither one of us looked away. It was like two badgers getting ready to mark their territory and our territory overlapped.

I elbowed one of the guys sitting with me and asked if he knew who the big guy was. He looked and confirmed he was at the motor transport school, but didn't know his name. He indicated everyone referred to him as "Scar Face"

I didn't see him again until the service support schools had a field meet which was where a military unit got together for a day of competition. There were several individual and team events scheduled. At that field meet, the events were geared toward physical fitness and military skills as opposed to team sports. Trophies were given out to the Marines who could do the most chin-ups, the most sit-ups in two minutes, and the person who could run the fastest three miles plus awards for the team that could erect a general-purpose tent the fastest. These erected tents were then used as base camp for all other events.

It was at the event called "Bull in the Ring" that I saw him again. Bull in the Ring is a favorite among Marines. It is basically a legal way to see who is the meanest and toughest Marine in a unit. It is a take-off of Japanese Sumo. Two people enter the ring that is six feet across; and whoever moves the other out, stays in the ring for the next challenger. Once you are pushed from the ring, you cannot go back in. You only get one chance as the "ringmaster." If you get moved out of the ring, you are through for that day's challenge. The game can be brutal; but it is also a crowd pleaser, especially for Marine Warriors.

This event, like most, has a strategy for winning. Don't go first. Try to wait until the end to participate. The person in the ring must go through others in order to stay in. The idea is to go through as few people as possible. The more people there are ahead of you, the better chance you have since the ringmaster will have been worn down. Normally, the guy and the biggest talk with the least something to back it up goes first.

As I suspected, all muscle and no brains Scar Face was standing the closest to the ring waiting for the event to begin. The school's executive officer called upon all contestants for the Bull in the Ring. Several Marines including me stepped toward the ring event.

The executive officer shouted with great flair, as if he were a barker at the circus, "Who will take the challenge to be the first in the Bull in the Ring?"

In response to this announcement, Scar Face jumped in the ring slapping his chest and screaming, "Nobody can move me out of this ring."

With an enthusiastic "OOH-RAH"—in Marine lingo, that's an answer for everything—he answered the call. He was taller than the six feet I had first estimated his stature to be. Now that I was closer, I guessed his height to be approximately 6' 2" and his weight at about 235 pounds. and he was as hard as Superman's kneecap. He was an ominous figure by anyone's standards, but with the scar, he was even more foreboding.

The executive officer, upon hearing the "OOH-RAH", turned to see who had accepted the challenge to be first in the ring. The crowd cheered as the executive officer acknowledged, "Private First Class Caesar Washington, get in the ring."

I thought to myself, "Caesar, what an appropriate name."

PFC Washington walked into the ring and stood there for a minute flexing his bicep and letting out a loud OOH-RAH.

The executive officer yelled, "Who will be the first challenger?"

A little guy who stood all of 5 feet 5 inches hollered a manly-sounding "OOH-RAH!" and the games began. The person running the ring, the executive officer, was responsible for setting up challengers. He was to ensure no rest period was provided to the ringmaster, but he didn't even have time to set up a new challenger before the little guy was thrown out of the ring. He might have stayed in the ring for all of 5 seconds.

The game continued and PFC Washington was invincible. Every challenger was quickly moved out of the ring. A few of the matches lasted for a minute, but most were over in the blink of an eye. I had great respect for his strength but was in awe of his endurance. Marine after Marine charged the ring, only to be quickly thwarted. Keeping in mind my strategy for winning the game, I waited until almost the very last person. At least one hundred Marines attempted to overthrow PFC Washington and control the ring. As soon as I stepped into the ring, Washington grabbed me like a man possessed. He had so much perspiration on him, he was hard to grab in return. I pulled away from him and then lunged headfirst, hoping I could run him backwards out of the ring. He picked me up in a bear hug, walked me to the edge of the ring, and threw me out. I must have flown at least three feet before I landed on my butt. PFC Washington went through the entire unit without being ousted. He was the true, "Bull in the Ring."

After a strenuous test of strength like that, I would have

been looking for the first shade in order to lie down and take a nap, but not PFC Washington. He and several of his friends headed over to the beer trailer. I watched him drink four beers in a matter of minutes. I know it was hot. He had just had a horrific workout, and he was perspiring like a thoroughbred horse.

I watched him, trying to understand why I was so consumed with him. I felt as if I had to prove myself to him, to let him know I was better than he was. To let him know I was in charge; and no matter how strong, physically or mentally he thought he was, I was better.

I was sitting under a general-purpose tent which had been erected earlier in the day. One of the senior non-commissioned officers walked by and I mentioned the number of beers Washington had consumed in such a short period of time.

The NCO said, "He's a big boy; I'm sure he knows what he is doing."

I watched Washington down a couple of more beers, and then someone brought him a couple of hot dogs from the grill. I felt better after I saw him eat something, but I thought that he had better slow down on those beers or he would find himself in trouble.

The word came to secure and go on liberty, once all equipment was properly stowed—a military word for "put away in the best condition possible from where it originally came."

Several of us planned on going into town and playing some pool. We quickly stored all the equipment and left. We went to the main hangout for single Marines in school. The place was nothing but dives and cheap businesses whose clientele were mainly young Marines who did not have a lot of money or brains to go anywhere else. It was where we could spend our money for very cheap thrills.

We had been downtown for a couple of hours when we

decided to get a pizza from the no-name pizza place at the end of the strip. As we were walking, we heard a ruckus in one of the dirtier, dingy watering holes. In the street listening to the commotion, one of the guys suggested we go in and see what was going on. As we collectively moved forward toward the door, a Marine came flying out.

We picked him up and he said, "Scar Face is tearing up the place. Come help us get him out of there before the owner calls the cops!"

Five of us walked into the place. I could see "Scar Face" Washington standing in the middle of the establishment with three Marines trying to take him down. The manager and/or owner, an Asian lady, was standing on the bar screaming, "Get him out of here now or I call the cops!"

We all moved rapidly but cautiously toward Scar Face. PFC Dave Jenkins from Dothan, Alabama, was the first one from my group to reach him. He tried to reason with him and tell him to calm down before he got himself in trouble. Scar Face already had a Marine on his right arm, one on his left arm, and another one wrapped around his legs trying to get him to the ground so they could tire him out or calm him down. Jenkins standing in front of him telling him to calm down was like waving a red blanket in front of a bull. Scar Face, with one big grunt, pushed the guy holding his right arm across the room and hit Jenkins right in the nose. Jenkins grabbed his face and fell backwards. I tried to catch him, but he went right through my hands. I stood over Jenkins as he sat up.

I said, "Let me see."

It was obvious his nose was broken for the blood was streaming down his lip and onto his clothes. All of us except Jenkins jumped on Scar Face and got him on the ground. With great difficulty, we were able to get him outside before the bar owner could call the police. We released him and ran, hoping he would run after us so we could get him back to the barracks. Jenkins was still inside the bar and I doubled back to see how badly he was hurt. I found him in the restroom, but the lights were dim and I couldn't see how badly he was hurt. All I could see was that blood was coming from his nose.

I grabbed some toilet paper and handed it to Jenkins. As he was cleaning himself up he asked me, "What did he hit me with?"

"His fist," I replied.

"That's the hardest I have ever been hit and I was a Golden Glove Boxer."

When we got outside there was no sign of the earlier struggle. Jenkins and I started back for base. As we got closer to the front gate, we could see a disturbance. Scar face was in handcuffs and the military police were taking statements.

When we reached the gate, one of the MPs asked Jenkins, "What happened to your nose?"

Jenkins didn't respond and the MP asked him again, "What happened to you nose?" this time a little more forcefully.

Jenkins pointed over at Scar Face and said, "We had a little run-in out in town, but it's okay. No harm done."

The MP told Jenkins he had to make a statement about what had happened. Jenkins started to protest, but the MP was a sergeant and told Jenkins that he had to do it. After Jenkins told them what happened, the MPs took him over to the clinic to be seen by a doctor. As I had already guessed, Jenkins' nose was broken. By the time he returned to the barracks two hours later, his eyes were black and blue, and starting to swell. Jenkins told me he would have to go back in the morning and be re-evaluated for a concussion.

The next morning Scar Face did not make formation

and was reported UA—Unauthorized Absence. We learned at breakfast that Washington had spent the night in the brig. Everyone was speculating about what would happen to him. One of the instructors told us not to worry about him. He explained military justice would be quick and fair.

Three days later, Scar Face went to officer hours which is similar to a civilian misdemeanor court. All of us who were in town and had witnessed the event were called to the Commanding Officer's office. I didn't think I was in trouble, but I was scared anyway. The Commanding Officer (CO) had the Sergeant Major call us into his office all at once and explained the procedures. He then explained the charges that PFC Washington faced. It was all very formal. I was beginning to feel somewhat at ease when the CO ordered PFC Washington to report. The Sergeant Major walked to the door and ordered PFC Caesar Washington to report to the Commanding Officer. Washington walked in handcuffed.

The CO asked him if he was going to behave himself if he had the handcuffs removed.

He responded, "Yes, sir."

"Remove the handcuffs," he ordered.

Like a father lecturing his own child, The CO explained the procedures and the authority which allowed him to perform these punitive duties; the charges which had been leveled against him; and the maximum punishment he could face. I felt sorry for "Scar Face" Washington, but understood the reasons behind the proceedings.

The CO asked Washington to explain what happened. Washington stated he couldn't remember. One by one the CO asked each of us what we had seen and heard on the night in question. One by one we provided details of the events. The CO listened as each individual he called upon provided information on the evening events and the broken nose of PFC Jenkins. As the last man finished his story, the CO started flipping through the Service Record Book, also known as the SRB, of PFC Washington.

The CO looked at one page for a long period of time and then called over the Sergeant Major. The CO pointed to a page in Washington's book and asked the Sergeant Major, "Is that the same one, you think?"

The Sergeant Major responded, "How many of them could there have possibly been?"

The CO stood from his chair with the Sergeant Major standing right next to him. He leaned over his desk resting his hands on the papers on top of the desk. He got as close as he could and whispered, "Washington, do you know a man by the name of Lincoln Grant Washington?"

Washington, who had been standing at the position of attention, appeared to go weak in the knees; and, with a crack in his voice answered, "Yes, sir. He was my father."

The CO looked directly into the eyes of Washington and said, "Was your father a Marine in Vietnam?

Again Washington responded, "Yes, sir."

The CO spoke with a different, sympathetic voice, "I understand you have paid a great sacrifice already. It must have been difficult for your mother rearing you boys by herself. If I let you go, will you promise to not let something like this happen again?"

Washington with great respect said, "Yes, sir!"

Without another word spoken and with the CO still leaning on his desk, he instructed the assembled group, "One of the first lessons any commander must learn is that forgiveness is always an option. PFC Jenkins, will you forgive PFC Washington for breaking your nose?"

Jenkins said, "Yes, sir!"

The CO continued, "Will everybody here forgive Washington for this indiscretion."

Everybody in unison replied, "Yes, sir!"

The CO stood up and said, "Washington, I find there to be mitigating circumstances concerning these office hours and these charges. I find these mitigating circumstances to excuse the charges against you and find you not guilty. You are free to go."

I was very happy for Washington because nothing can be sadder than a Marine losing a stripe. They are very hard to come by, and to lose one can be devastating. It was a solemn moment for everyone.

However, those proceedings opened up a dialog for a whole new group of questions which needed to be answered.

Who is or was Washington's father?

You could tell Washington was happy to have been found not guilty at the office-hours, but time and mission did not allow any of us the time to get our many questions about Washington answered.

CHAPTER 9

The Assignments

I lost track of Washington after he graduated shortly after the office hours, and I did not get my questions about his father answered. I continued with supply school, graduated sixth out of thirty-six, and got my first Fleet Marine Force (FMF) assignment. You weren't considered a real Marine until you had served in the FMF.

My first assignment was Okinawa, Japan, and was exactly what I was hoping for. I wanted to go overseas, visit foreign countries, and see different cultures. I couldn't believe my luck. Most of the others in my class were being ordered to Camp LeJuene about twelve miles up the road. I had already been to LeJuene and there was nothing there. I wanted something different and I got it. I don't know how I got so lucky. Others in the class were just as excited that they *didn't* get overseas tours.

At graduation, everyone said their good-byes and parted ways. Those who were staying at LeJeune didn't have the opportunity for leave; but those going overseas received another ten days of leave just as we had when we graduated from boot camp. I was so excited about going overseas that I declined the leave in order to get to Okinawa sooner.

It was the first part of June when I arrived on Okinawa, commonly referred to as "the rock." It was a Thursday. When the crew opened the doors to the plane, two things became readily apparent. One, it was hot and humid; and two, the air had a displeasing, pungent odor. The salty Gunnery Sergeant who had slept—and snored—next to me on the plane took in a deep breath through his nostrils and said with a grin on his face, "Nothing like the smell of a crematorium."

I ask him, "What's a crematorium?"

"They don't bury people here, they burn them. The place where they burn human remains is called a crematorium and they always burn the remains on Thursdays."

The year I spent on Okinawa was certainly an eye-opening experience, not only in my military career, but also in learning a different culture. I was having a great time and felt life could get no better.

When most of the Marines I billeted with were going into town to have a few drinks, I was going on walking tours of the World War II battle sites. When my buddies were going to the movies, I was learning how to SCUBA dive. When they were sleeping off hangovers, I was at the gym working out. I had a great role model in my non-commissioned officer. Corporal Marcus K. Donahue was a black Marine from Brooklyn, New York, who firmly believed that partaking of alcohol served no useful purpose in life. He went to college during his off-duty hours; he read constantly; and was the epitome of physical fitness and mental agility. When he spoke, one could tell he was educated. I wanted to be like him. He helped me to get into college; took me on some of the World War II Battle Tours; gave me a few books to read; and was really a great mentor. He provided a great foundation on which I could build my military career.

When I departed Okinawa, I received orders to report to the Commanding General, 2nd Marine Division, Camp LeJeune, North Carolina. I had already been to Camp Lejeune and didn't want to go back. Cpl Donahue heard me complaining so he pulled me aside and gave me some very insightful information. He said, "Look, idiot. This is the Marine Corps. We are small. There are only so many places you can go. Go and be a flower even if you are planted in the crack of a sidewalk."

I asked myself out loud, "What does that mean? Be a flower in the cement?"

I must have had a confused and dazed looked on my face because he explained, "No matter where you go in the Corps, bloom wherever you are planted." He continued, "It doesn't matter what job you have, who you work for, or where you are stationed, the only way to get ahead and stay ahead is to have a great attitude and do the very best job you can. Those for whom you work will take notice and take care of you."

These words have never failed me. I took his advice to heart and time has proven that he was correct. I often think of where I would be today if not for Corporal Donahue teaching and guiding me through this time in my life.

When I arrived at Camp LeJeune, I was assigned to the 24th Marine Expeditionary Unit, known as the 24th MEU. As I was checking into the unit, I met some of the guys from boot camp and classmates from supply school. We talked about some of the guys who had graduated with us and eventually the name Washington came up. One of the guys said there was a Lance Corporal Washington attached to the 24th MEU over in the motor pool. Could it be the same guy? With this information we all turned and asked, "What does he look like?"

He described the physical attributes of Washington precisely including the scar. He was now a Lance Corporal and worked in the motor pool as a mechanic. I said to myself, "It has been a little over a year. I was a corporal about to be promoted to sergeant or, as we called it, "pinning-on" sergeant. I was certain it was the same Washington I had known from school.

This question was answered within the next second. As we continued to talk, Washington walked into the barracks. Everyone enthusiastically greeted him. It was obvious he was popular or else everyone was scared of him and wanted to be his friend. He greeted everybody standing around. When he started meeting all the new guys, he shook everyone's hand and introduced himself. When he got to me, he looked in my eyes and remembered me from our school days.

He said, "I remember you."

There was a definite change in the tone of his voice. I don't know what it was, but I could tell he looked and talked to me differently than the others he had just met. I wasn't the only one who noticed the difference. One of the other Marines who had checked in with me earlier in the day asked, "Do you know him? It sure seems like he knows you." I quickly explained our earlier meeting and let it go.

Everyone in the unit was really excited. Being with the MEU meant going on a float. This would be a great time. One got to ride on US Navy ships and pull into ports around the world; conduct war fighting training; and then had a few days of liberty before pulling out to go to the next port to repeat the training cycle, and hopefully performing the mission/training and having better liberty than the time before.

As we were preparing for the float and to conduct this war-fighting training, we got called up to perform peacekeeping actions in a place called the Middle East. They told us where it was, but I had never heard of the place.

There were mixed reactions among the Marines when we received word of the mission. Many did not like it because it meant we would go to only one place and stay, not go to different "ports of call." Others thought it would be boring just sitting around all day guarding a post and showing our forces as a deterrent to anyone who wanted to gnash their teeth. Others thought it was good because peacekeeping was considered a relatively safe operation. For every Marine attached to the unit, a different opinion could be heard. The politics and philosophy of war fighting and peacekeeping were the responsibilities of the officers. All the enlisted had to do was follow orders. As I had heard many times before, "They don't pay enlisted people to think".

I tried to take Corporal Donahue's advice to heart one more time and "just bloom wherever the Corps planted me, even if I landed in a crack in the sidewalk."

When we arrived at the new place, things were understandably confusing. Everyone was trying to understand the mission and the roles we played as "Marine Peacekeepers." We were living in a barracks not far from the city. I was in a logistical support role, but every Marine is a "basic rifleman." Everyone had to pull duty on the perimeter gates. It didn't matter if you were an infantryman (affectionately called a "grunt") or a cook, everyone had to pull duty. I could tell by the reactions of some of the more seasoned Marines that they were not happy with the rules of engagement and/or the security plan for guarding the compound.

It was obvious the officers and Staff Non-Commissioned Officers were uneasy with our security situation at the barracks, but they did the very best they could with what few assets were available. We peons heard the officers talking of how they had repeatedly asked for additional equipment to assist with personnel protection, but their requests had been turned down.

Those in the higher headquarters had said, "We are here on a strictly peacekeeping mission and we don't want to be seen as an aggressor."

I certainly didn't understand the politics or the decisions. I was way down the food chain, and I didn't have a clue about the political decisions that were being made. I certainly didn't know what was going on in the closed-door sessions, but everyone could tell the leadership on the ground was not happy. They frequently made visits to the various posts to ensure everyone was always alert and knew what to do in case of an emergency. Neither they nor anyone else understood what was going on or what to do to improve the situation. I, like most of the guys, was too dumb to ask questions. We just hoped those in the leadership positions knew what they were doing and would do it well.

Early one morning in late October of 1983, the Duty Non-Commissioned Officer woke me up as I had requested. I had been assigned as the Sergeant of the Guard and I needed to check the post with the off-going Sergeant of the Guard. As I was getting dressed, now Corporal Washington walked into my area and said the vehicle was ready. He had been assigned as the duty driver for the day.

As I finished putting on my boots, I bumped the rack. My bunkmate woke up and said, "I'm awake! I'm not sleeping!" I patted him on the shoulder, apologized, and told him to go back to sleep. I am sure he was still asleep, because he responded, "A Marine on duty has no friends."

I walked outside the barracks and could smell the coffee from the chow hall. Washington was waiting for me so I got in the vehicle and we headed for breakfast. We didn't say a word to each other on the way. When we got to the makeshift parking lot, we went inside and got two bananas. Private Washington got two thermos cans of coffee and one of hot soup.

When he jumped back into the vehicle, I offered him a banana. His response surprised me, "Not all monkeys eat bananas." I could tell he was angry.

"What are you mad about?" I asked.

"You ain't got a clue, do you?" he said.

"No, why don't you explain it to me?" I responded.

This was the first time that I had gotten the opportunity to talk to Washington about who he was, what he wanted out of life, what his future plans were, how he got the scar on his face, and most importantly who his father was. Our conversation continued, but it was strained. I told him bananas were all they had that I could grab in a hurry and again offered him one of the bananas. He reluctantly took it and starting eating.

As we starting driving to the guard shacks, I tried to get him to say why he was so angered. He talked about the Marines and the peacekeeping mission we had been handed, about the security of the area, the lack of support both logistically and medically, and why the officers weren't doing a better job of correcting the obvious deficiencies. He discussed the politics of the day and why they were leaving us to the mercy of the local nationals. (I didn't know who "they" were, but he was on a roll and I didn't want to stop him from talking.) He asked why we couldn't put up a more defensive posture. We are sitting ducks or fish in a barrel just asking for trouble. It was obvious Washington had been thinking deeply about our situation. I, on the other hand, had been sitting around fat, dumb, and happy; oblivious to any of the problems he mentioned.

As we checked post, the Marines were alert and ready to move on any target at a moment's notice. Most of them asked about live rounds. We had guards without bullets. Trying to explain to a trained trigger-hugger that peacekeepers do not require bullets is as difficult as explaining the color blue to a person who has been blind all his life. It is impossible. We continued to check post and tried to bring as much comfort to the guards as possible.

I told Washington that he obviously had thought a lot about

our precarious situation, and I asked what made him think so deeply about it.

He stated, "Based on what I have been told, the same thing happened to my father and his unit in Vietnam. I don't want us to learn his unit's lesson all over again."

I told Washington I was very interested in his father's situation and the lessons learned by his father's unit and wanted to hear about it. He told me since we would be together all day he would tell me while we stood the duty. Finally, I would get a chance to know why the Commanding Officer let Washington free on the earlier charges.

Washington pulled the vehicle up to the back hatch of the barracks. He said he would take the thermos bottles back to the chow hall and that he would meet me in the duty hut once he had turned them in.

As he started to drive away I asked, "Would you tell me about your face and that scar?"

He laughingly said it was an embarrassing and stupid story, but he would tell me.

The old sergeant of the guard wanted to go to the chow hall, too. He and Washington took off in the vehicle as I started up the back steps to the door leading into the barracks.

As I got to the back hatch of the barracks, I heard Marines at the front of the barracks yelling and screaming. I could tell from the tone in their screams that there were problems, just as a mother knows from her child's screams whether the child is hurt and how badly.

If I had been a comic book hero my spider senses would have been tingling. For the first time in my life, I was scared and I was on the defensive. In my mind, I reviewed everything I'd learned in military training; and, for some reason, I drew my pistol.

I started back down the stairs to go around front to see if I could assist with the problem. I was practically down to the last step when it happened. A suicide bomber drove through the front gate of the compound; drove up the front steps of the barracks; and blew everything up. Later I learned that the building was all but destroyed. Many of the men were still asleep and had no opportunity to defend themselves. There was no warning so many of them had no idea what hit them. It was a cold, calculated strike—a senseless and cowardly thing to do.

I remember hearing a loud noise; but then I must have momentarily passed out because when I woke up, dust was still thick in the air and I could not breathe. I thought it was due to the dust. I wanted to wave my hands in front of my face and try to get some clean air so I could get a breath; however, my hands were trapped beneath me. I was on the ground. I was trying to move my head but I could not.

From what I could see, I was in a huge pile of debris with a metal support beam lying across my face. A large part of an exterior wall had fallen and was lying on my body. My back must have been arched, because my head was turned and I could see a boot. It was in the air, up the stairs I had just been running down. My head rested on the ground, and I was doing everything possible to get some air.

The wall was so heavy it was literally crushing me to death. I was trying to thrash around and free myself, but quickly realized that I needed to calm down and think. I could hear myself trying to breathe, but the wall was just too heavy. My arms were trapped and I could not move. I looked around as best I could for anyone who could help. I didn't want to cry out for help and waste what air I had left. I started to let the air slowly leave my lungs. I wanted to see if the wall would continue to crush me or if it was stable. Was it resting against me or something else?

Every time I let out a little air, the wall just continued to fall and crush me. I was hoping it would stay in place and allow me to breathe. No such luck.

Think, man, think! After another few seconds of thrashing around trying fruitlessly to get out from under the wall, I prayed, *"God, please don't let me die here, not like this."*

I could tell my time was coming to an end. I was starting to get tunnel vision. I was afraid I wouldn't last much longer from lack of oxygen just as I had heard pilots talk about.

At that moment, like an angel's voice, I heard Washington shout, "Sergeant, are you okay? Can you hear me?"

I couldn't see him and evidently he couldn't see my face. I knew he was talking to me because I could feel him tapping on the wall that had me pinned down.

He screamed, "I see your feet. Can you move your feet?" I wanted him to know I was still alive so I did everything I could to ensure my feet were moving. It must have worked because he said, "Good, good! Give me a moment and I'll try and get you out."

All I could think was "you'd better hurry." I could hear some debris being moved but it was slow. I knew if he didn't go faster, I would be gone. Then Washington did the worst thing possible, I thought. He walked across the wall that had me pinned down. As he got to the other side of the wall, he jumped. As he jumped, the wall bounced just a little; but it was enough for me to get half a breath of air. It was so sweet, dust and all. I heard some more debris being thrown from the pile. The whole time Washington was screaming words of encouragement. "Hang on just another minute! Don't give up! Give me another moment!"

Washington again walked over the wall and jumped off the side; and again, the bounce provided another slight breath of air.

I still couldn't see him, but I could tell Washington was working as hard as he could to get me out from under the wall.

He hollered, "Hey, I gotta go get something that can give me some leverage, I can't move this thing by myself. Hang on for just another minute. I'll be right back!"

What seemed like an eternity could have only been just a few seconds.

When Washington returned, he told me, "I got a metal pipe. I am going to try and lift the wall. Get ready to climb out if you can. On three, Okay? One, two, three!" Washington let out a massive roar as he pushed on the metal pipe. The wall moved just a little and I got another breath of air. Washingtor. screamed as the wall came down on me again.

I could hear Washington breathing heavily; but a few seconds later he cried out as if he were in agony, "One more time, on three." Washington again let out a roar and pushed the wall moving it up a few inches. This time I was able to get a big breath and turn a little on my side.

Much to my horror, I saw that I was lying in a pool of blood. I was not a medical expert, but I could tell by the color of the blood and the skin that had already formed on the blood that I was hurt and hurt badly. While Washington continued to work on the debris pile and the wall, my mind was racing. "Where is the nearest hospital ship? Is there a doctor on the compound or is he in the rubble? The clinic was on the first deck of the barracks. No doubt about it, the Corpsmen, doctors and any medical personnel were probably gone. How long would it take to get a "med-i-vac" helicopter to the barracks?" My thoughts went from suffocation to bleeding to death in a split second.

I pulled my attention back to what Washington was doing. He was now moving debris with his hands and, though my hands were somewhat free, I could offer no assistance. Washington grabbed the medal post again and I could feel the metal support beam lying across my face start to move. Washington screamed again, "I think I can get you now. Let me push one more time and see what we can do."

I was praying that I had enough strength to pull myself out; but, with all that blood loss, I couldn't be sure.

Again, he counted, "One, two, three!" and screamed again as if he were in tremendous pain. The wall moved and cracked in the middle. When the wall cracked, Washington was able to lift a large portion of the wall up allowing me to crawl out.

I started crawling through the enormous pool of blood. It was enormous. I knew I wouldn't be able to make it to the hospital ship, of having lost so much blood.

I crawled out on all fours and looked down to see where the blood was coming from. Could I apply a tourniquet to an arm or leg to stop the bleeding? I might lose the limb, but at least save my life. I checked my arms. They were covered in blood, but no wounds that would have caused this type of blood loss. I checked my legs—bloody, but again, no serious wounds that would have caused that much loss of blood. Body nothing; head nothing. Where was all that blood coming from?

Then I thought, *My God, there's someone else is in the pile!*

Still on all fours, I turned to Washington and screamed, "Washington, there must be someone else in here! Look at all this blood!" I moved some of the large pieces of debris, trying to see if I could find someone.

I noticed Washington wasn't helping. Without looking up I shouted, "Washington, there is someone else in here. Help me get him out!"

No sooner had I said that than I heard a thud. Washington lay on the ground ten feet in front of me.

I shouted, "Washington, what are you doing?"

Still feeling quite wobbly, I stood up and walked over to him. He was lying on his left side facing the wall he had just moved off me toward the barracks.

I hollered, "Washington, what's wrong!" I knelt down beside him and turned him over on his back.

As he completed the roll he was smiling and said, "You're okay, but I told you. Just like my father in Nam, we had to learn this lesson all over again.

It took my eyes a second to adjust. When they did, I saw that Washington's left arm had been blown completely off his shoulder. The blood, which I had been lying in, wasn't mine. It was his.

Made in the USA
Charleston, SC
14 May 2013